PUNISHERS AND OPPRESSORS

Punishers and Oppressors

ALDIVAN TORRES

aldivan teixeira torres

CONTENTS

1

"PUNISHERS AND OPPRESSORS"

Aldivan Torres
Punishers and oppressors

Author: Aldivan Torres
©2018- Aldivan Torres
All rights reserved

Aldivan Torres is an advertising, banker and graphic designer. Literature is a fun and a leisure that leads you to the best feelings. For life, democracy, and freedom is always his motto.

"Punishers and oppressors"
2.54-Inauguration
2.55-Punisher in action
2.56-A week later

2.54-INAUGURATION

Dawns. Still early, those responsible for the project wake up, get up and prepare everything in detail to avoid undesirable surprises. At approximately 08:00 A.M. they were ready to start the arduous task of running a business without much experience. But what mattered was that they were ready to fight for him.

When they open their doors, they come across a good number of people, the result of the work done by Angel in the village a week before. Cheerful and with a smile on their face, the two partners welcome visitors. At the time, present the premises of the place, products, and prices into account captivated customers. This strategy seems to work because the movement is intense throughout the morning.

When they close for lunch, they make a quick assessment of their efforts and the result is positive. They agree by common agreement to continue with mass dissemination not only in the village but also in neighboring sites and villages because as the saying "Propaganda is the soul of business" says.

A moment later, they're going to lunch. This is a pleasurable moment of intense family union lasting about thirty minutes. After, get some rest. In the afternoon, they reopen the market. As in the morning, the movement is good and the talent of the sellers is praised. Much of the stock is sold at the end of the day.

At exactly 18:00 Hour's work is closed. Even without taking stock, Angel and Victor are very optimistic. In fact, it had been a genius idea to open a venture in the thriving village of Carabais despite great competition.

Finally, for the first time in his life, Vítor could have a better quality of life after years of intense work in precarious agriculture. All this thanks to the trust of the Magellan family. Specifically, in Angel's person. Even though I loved him, He didn't mix business with feelings.

It was the beginning of a new era for everyone.

2.55-PUNISHER IN ACTION

A week has passed. He'd be home on Sunday. It was the day agreed for the reunion between the group of vigilantes who had as a new center of action the village of Carabais. At 9:00 a.m., everyone was already present at Angel's new address. Scattered in a circle across the room, attention turned to the boss who had something important to say. Then he pronounces:

"My friends, a decisive time is coming. From now on, we need to stay focused early and be more rigid. This, in my opinion, is extremely necessary. (Angel)

"I get it. What's the next step, master? (Raphael)

"Let us not submit to the force opposed to our own. We need to stop the dismantling of Mr. Soares who is the head of the region's elites. (Angel)

"What would be our first target? (Interested Victor)

"Free the poor peasants trapped a fortnight ago in the dungeon of the farm for rebelling. (Angel)

"What about resistance? They say they're watched all the time. (Wanted to know Penelope)

"If we're in good numbers, we have a chance. (Angel)

"It's all right. Even if we know our strength, we have to be careful. (Ricardo noted)

"Am I going to have to go this time? (Marcela)

"Well, I chose for this mission Raphael, Richard, and Penelope. Any impositions? (Angel)

"No. You're the one who knows master. Isn't that personal? (Opined Victor)

"Yes. (The others)

"When are we going? (Raphael)

"Right now. The others are in training with me. (The Master)

"That's all right. See you later. Let's go? Ricardo and Penelope? (Raphael)

"Let's go, let's go. (both)

After the farewell, the three designated forwarded the exit. Anxious, nervous and expectant go over the door and access the outside. From then on, they headed north of the village. In the surroundings, the imposing head of the Carabais farm was located.

As it was morning, they decided to become invisible in order to go unnoticed by the obstacles of the way. Until arrival at the place of the place, it is successful in a total of twenty minutes. However, as they approach the dungeon, they are detected by opponents who were also three (Orlando, Patricia and Clementina).

Then a fight begins between them. Each one catches his opponent. Unlike other times, evil mutants take advantage because they use black magic as their new weapon. In the end, they manage to reject the attempt at liberation.

Even sad, the mutants of good give up the operation because they realize that they were not prepared to face this new reality. They retreat in order to find a solution to this new problem.

They begin the return journey. On the way, they were looking for explanations for what happened. How did you fail even though you tried so hard? The sense of disappointment was too great. Crests, they arrive at the precinct giving the bad news.

"We can't do it. Can you believe that? (Rafael Vents)

"It's possible. How did you lose? (Angel)

"It was very strange. Despite my development, it seemed that my powers were blocked. I don't know what happened. (Ricardo reported)

"If I were there, we'd win. (Commented Vítor)

"Don't be proud. It would be the same. I think they used heavy black magic this time. (Angel)

"That's right, that's right. I've heard them summon the demon's name several times. (Penelope)

"What a fear! Now what do we do? (Marcela)

"Well, I'm in doubt. If we use white magic, we can balance the dispute. But victory will depend on details. (Angel)

"How about we know the other side? With the science of your weaknesses, we can use this to our advantage. (Victor)

"A good idea, but the price is high. Who would qualify for that role? (Angel)

"I'm myself. I've always wanted to know a little from the left and I think this was the ideal opportunity. Any suggestions? (Victor)

"I've heard a lot about the healer. He is a master of darkness who has denied his beliefs. Couldn't he help? (Marcela)

"What do you think, master? (Victor)

"It's a possibility, but if you agree to be trained by him, it's at your own risk, understand? (Angel)

"I believe you, brother. (Raphael)

"I will try, for the good of all and for our greater focus. Where can I find him, Marcela? (Victor)

"On the Painted site. I went once and I'll take you there if you want. (Marcela)

"All right. Next Sunday, we're going. Any objections? (Victor)

"No, none. I admire your courage. (Angel)

"Great Victor! (Ricardo exclaimed)

"Well, for now, you're dismissed. Let's get back to our activities. (Angel)

Each one was saying goodbye and heading to their respective destination. What's next? What would happen? Let's keep up with the facts.

2.56-A WEEK LATER

After the failed attempt to liberate the peasants by the mutants of the good, another week began with it going without further surprises: the work to promote the market of light (name of the enterprise opened by Angel) were intensified, the mutants engaged in their respective works, the romantic pair Marcela-Ricardo remained firm and strong, the Torres family (Filomena and Rafael) and Magellan (Parents of Angel) remained on the site acting in various directions.

Arriving on Sunday, as promised, Marcela arrived in Carabais. Specifically, in front of Victor's residence. By knocking firmly on the door, he expects to be answered. A few moments later, the host greets her, greets her and takes the initiative in the conversation:

"Good morning, I've been waiting for you. Ready to reveal to me what I need? (Victor)

"Yes. And you, ready? (Marcela)

"Well, in the current situation, I don't think I have much choice. Let's see how it goes. (Victor)

"There's always a choice. But if you want, we can go. (Marcela)

"That's right, that's right. Wait a minute while I'm going to pack my backpack. (Victor)

"Yes, of course. (Marcela)

Victor entered the house for a few moments heading to his room. In this enclosure, the room took your backpack. Then he went to the kitchen and filled it with supplies. When everything was ready, the decided exit was headed again. The fact that his wife was traveling made things easier. Meeting Marcela again, he gave a positive signal that together they would begin to walk the journey. Then they both left.

Already out, restless, Vítor inquires his travel partner to get additional information.

"Where is the painted site located?

"It's very close to here. Maximum twenty minutes' walk. (Marcela)

"I get it. How does the healer present himself? (Victor)

"Easy. You'll have all the answers at the right time. You better get to know him and draw your own conclusions. (Marcela)

"That's all right. Thank you. (Victor)

A few meters ahead, after walking through the village houses, they took the south direction. Victor tried not to bother his friend anymore. With each step they took they approached the hope of refacing against opponents who were engaged in the destruction of their goals. Would it be worth fighting fire with fire? Let's continue the narrative.

As anticipated by Marcela, after twenty minutes of wandering between previously unknown paths, they arrived at a small hut made of crossed sticks and clay with straw cover.

At this point, Marcela says goodbye explaining that she had a pending issue with Angel. Greet him with a kiss on his face and leave. What's next? The young Victor would have to go on alone, full of doubts, fear and about to discover a little what fate revealed. What's to be done?

Without much thought, he advances toward the entrance. Touching the wooden door knocks slightly apprehensive. In seconds, she is attended to by a young man, about her age, rickety, slender, light brown and of well-defined features. Unsurprisingly, he starts the conversation.

"How's it going young? Willing to fight?

"Yes. But how do you know? (Victor)

"I know a lot of things. But don't ask yet how. Victor's your name, isn't it? (Healer)

"Yes, and yours? (Victor)

"Sorry. I've been mastering this name since I changed my life, and I suppose you came here to ask for help against the darkness, making me relive this phase of my life. (Healer)

"That's exactly what I'm going to do but if you don't want to help, I'll understand. (Victor)

"Easy. Let's not get ahead of ourselves. Tell me a little about yourself. I'm interested. (Healer)

"Well, I'm a native of the Fundão's Place. I belong to the Torres family and from a young age I try to meet my destiny. I have a gift: I'm a psychic. On this path, I met several people who helped me. I learned a lot, loved, I was disappointed, I found love again, I got married, I settled on work and the group I'm part of. For all "I love, I'm here wanting to react to the oppression of darkness. Who are you? (Victor)

"I'm from Bahia and I ended up here because my parents passed away. I had an aunt here, who also passed away. I'm alone today. (Healer)

"Exactly what are you? What are your powers? (Victor)

"Many consider me a wizard. Others, a monk. There are even some who suspect I'm an alien. In fact, it's all just a rumor. I'm a healer. I know the secret of plants and I am one of the few people who master the secret of the two forces. (Healer)

"I get it. Can you help me? (Victor)

"It depends. What do you want to provoke? (Healer)

"I want to know a way to be immune to black magic. Or at least fight toe-to-toe. (Victor)

"It's interesting. But it won't be easy. Do you intend to split up? (Healer)

"What do you mean? (Victor)

"I'll explain. By passing on to you my knowledge, you are implicitly accepting the spiritual dispute between the two forces for your soul. Depending on the moment, you may lose your soul forever. (Warned the Healer)

"I'm aware. I'll do what you ask. (Victor)

"Request accepted. Come in and talk a little bit more. (Healer)

Victor accepted the invitation and both entered the humble residence. Observing the environment, Victor noted the great religiosity of that man demonstrated in the statues and pictures of saints beyond the good taste of the few furniture. In a single span, everything was very simple. Gently, the host offered him a stool and sat on another. They stood in front of each other and then the dialogue can be resumed.

"First, congratulations on the simplicity. How is your day to day basically? (Victor)

"Thank you, thank you. As a healer, I live to care for my plants alone except for the company of my saints. Despite the rumors, I don't hurt anyone these days. On the contrary, I try to help those who come to me as best I can. (Healer)

"Why do you say it these days? You've done a lot of harm in the old day? (Victor)

"I must confess that I do. However, I regretted and was re-born as a human being. This dark period is usually called the "Dark Night of the Soul" and even the Saints experience it. But it's over. (Healer)

"With regard to love, have you tried it? (Victor)

"No, not yet. Neither love nor sincere friendship. However, since I'm still young I have time for a first time. (Healer)

"When your aunt died, you didn't want to return to Bahia? (Victor)

"No, I like it here. I identified with the people and the place. So much so that I consider myself a backing-back shoot, a region the world has forgotten. Changing the subject, tell me a little more about yourself now. In addition to coping with black magic, what other goals do you want to achieve with my help? (Healer)

"I want to dominate the left. Get to know your strengths and weaknesses in depth. Anyway, knowledge without involvement. I want to be a master like you. (Victor)

"All right. Goal. However, it is a long way to go, a "Great Crossing". In it, you will discover a little more of yourself, the universe, God, the Devil, fate, and how to use free will at the right time. When he arrives, you will find the peace and happiness so desired. (Healer)

"I get it. When do we start? (Victor)

"If there is no hindrance on your part, right now. I'm going to teach you how to protect yourself from black magic. (Healer)

"No, none. You can start. (Victor)

At this point, an owl shuddered near the hovel and the healer shuddered. Instinctively, he hit the wood of the stool on which Victor was sitting and crossed his arms. Shorty, warned:

"This is a bad sign. Some fallen spirit must be lurking. Come with me. (Healer)

Victor obeyed the master. Together they walked to a lake near the hut. Arriving at the edge, the healer knelt down and asked the disciple to do the same. Then prayed silently filling both hands with water and offered it to his partner. Even though he was not secure, Victor took it. At the end, the conversation resumed.

"That's it, that's it. Those who drink from this water and learn the prayer I will teach have no problems with the performance of inferior spirits. Do you believe that? (Healer)

"Yes, if you're talking. (Victor)

"That's not what I wanted to hear. Do you really believe in your heart? (Healer)

For a moment, Victor thought a little watching around. He contemplated the universe in every way. Yes, I had to agree that anything was possible and that there were many mysteries in the world even though it seemed absurd. Then, raising his head he faced the teacher proclaiming:

"Yes, I believe! (Victor)

"All right. Congratulations. (Praised the healer)

"Teach me prayer. (Victor)

"Yes, of course. You must pray like this: Blessed geniuses of light, I invoke you in my personal protection. It holds my body and soul from my enemies. Let no evil being can harm me or approach me. I force you in the name of Jesus Christ, the lion of David. So be it.

"That's it? (Victor)

"Yes, isn't that simple? However, it only suits you and you won't be able to teach anyone. Understood? (Healer)

"That's good. What's the next step? (Victor)

"We have six more to fulfill. However, it has to be on alternate days. How about you book in a month, always on Sunday? (Healer)

"That's great. It's the only day I don't work on the market. (Victor)

"Then it's right that way. A month from now, we'll meet, and I'm asking for your discretion as to everything you've seen and heard here. For today, you're clear. (Healer)

"Thank you and until another time. (Victor)

"See you later. (Healer)

With a handshake, they finally say goodbye. While the healer returns to the hut, Victor heads to the village of Carabais. It would be another 20-minute walk. Only this time it would be quieter because the meeting resolves several doubts of yours. Let's move on then.

2.57-FAMILY REUNION

Upon arriving and entering the house, Vítor comes to the visit of his family members (Filomena, Rafael, and little Clara). Surprised and delighted, they greet each other with kisses and hugs after a long breakup time.

They gather in the room to kill their homesickness with a good conversation. Except Penelope is preparing lunch after returning from travel.

"How's my mother? (Victor)

"In the usual struggle, doing domestic and craft activities. When I have a break, I'm going to go for a walk at the house of relatives and friends like today. And you, my son, all right? (Filomena)

"I'm satisfied. In the professional area, I'm learning a lot in the new business. In the personal area, I am happy with my wife and with the initial learning with my new master. (Said Vítor)

"You mean you put your idea into practice? A lot of courage from you. (Rafael noted)

"Who doesn't risk, don't snack, dear brother. Besides, we have to think about the good of our group first. (Victor)

"I missed you brother. Why did you disappear? (Babbled Clara)

"Don't you remember, little one? Married. (Explained Vítor)

"But you didn't have to part with us. I'm mad at Penelope! (Clara)

"No, don't feel that. She's a great person. (Raphael)

"You have me and your brother Raphael. (Completed Filomena)

"That's right. Don't you remember what you said one day? Together always even if it's in spirit. (Argued Victor)

"Okay! (Clara)

"Please, Clara, go play outside. The three of us now need to have a conversation between adults. (Suggested Filomena)

"I've known! Adults, so complicated...... (Clara)

Kind of mumbling, Clara walked away and headed for the exit. When the conversation was at a safe distance, the conversation resumed.

"Well, now that we're alone, could you explain what this story is about donating to the group? (Filomena was interested)

"No big deal, Mom. I take all the necessary care not to get too involved. (Victor)

"I think it's good. If you or your brother are hiding something from me, you're going to see me later. (Alerted Filomena)

"It's nothing. You can rest assured. Isn't that Rafael? (Victor)

"Yes, of course. You can trust me. (Raphael)

Now, Penelope approaches announcing that lunch is ready. Everybody's heading for the kitchen. Except Filomena who's going to call Clara outside the house. Five minutes later, the two returns and join the rest of the group.

Then, in a mild atmosphere, the family lunch begins. For twenty-five minutes, between conversations, exchange of kindnesses and healthy intrigues, participants have the opportunity to feel the taste of belonging to the Towers. That simple family, however, of honest, dignified and hardworking people. The nickname of seers was represented in the generation by the incredible Victor.

After lunch, they carry out other social and leisure activities throughout the afternoon. They only get apart near nightfall. In farewell, emotion takes over everyone, and they commit to seeing each other from time to time in their busy and troubled lives.

When they finally get apart, Victor, for the first time on the day, he's alone with his wife. Before anything goes wrong, take the opportunity to have a little more intimacy with her. At the climax of pleasure, he thinks: How nice it was to have married! Actually, this was one of the advantages of being married. On the other hand, responsibilities increased because he was head of the family. However, until now, he was matching expectations.

After the act of pleasure, they went to dinner. At the time, one shares with the other the news of the day. Among them, there were hardly any secrets. After, they leave a little and will contemplate the immensity of the universe staying in this exercise about two hours. At the end of this time, they get tired and go to sleep. The next day they would continue their normal activities.

The working week started normally. Since early days, after a reinforced breakfast, the young couple formed by the mutants Penelope and Vítor was taking the most in domestic activities and in the service in the market. They were doing very well, by the way.

Lunch was ready early. The people who went to buy in the establishment were met with promptness and delicacy as they deserved. The balance was quite positive in every way.

At the end of the day, a good surprise: They met three young women named Adelina Maciel, Celia Alonso and Henrietta Soares. The latter, the Colonel's son. This meeting served to strengthen ties and to demystify the concept they had of the Soares family. At least one was saved.

After much talk, they booked a visit for a weekend at Adelina's house in a month at most. Everyone promised to be there and go out for a while wouldn't do any harm to the couple. On the contrary, it would only add experience.

They finally said goodbye. They closed their hours and returned home. Furthermore, they dined, made love and other activities common to a couple of those at the time. Early on, they went to sleep because the other day would be quite full.

One day, it happened. As he had already begun his new path and felt prepared to act, Victor called an extraordinary meeting between him, Angel, Marcela, and Ricardo. It was the most powerful quartet among the mutants of good.

In the late afternoon, everyone arrived gathering rushing at Angel's house behind closed doors. In the respective seats of the room, they settled and the conversation was initiated by the one who provoked the meeting.

"Well, in case you haven't already known, I've begun to submit to the healer's teachings. I will go all the way for me and for everyone. (Victor)

"It's all right. I hope you don't regret it later. (Angel)

"Don't worry, master. I won't forget what I've learned from you if that's what makes you afraid. (Victor)

"At what price? (Ricardo)

"I can't reveal it. But you can rest assured. I know what I'm doing. (Assured Vítor)

"What have you learned? (Marcela)

"In this first contact, to stay out of the influence of inferior spirits. I believe that with my help we can finally free the peasants. What do you think? (Victor)

"That's a good idea. How many do you need to help him? (Angel)

"I think me, Ricardo and Marcela are enough. Together, we can succeed. Are we together? (Victor)

"Of course. Count me in. (Ricardo)

"With me, too. (Marcela)

"That's fine with me, too. One for all and all for one! (Angel)

"For the wronged! (Ricardo)

"For the right thing! (Marcela)

"And carefully! (Victor)

After saying goodbye to the master, the trio immediately went to the Carabais farm's headland. On the way, they become invisible and with twenty minutes of vigorous walking already approach the dungeon where the peasants are locked.

After a few more meters are detected by opponents who are in three as well. This time you have to fight Romeo (Gift of strength), Helium (power over fire) and Clementine (Climate).

Then a new fight begins. The pairs formed are: Vítor versus Clementina, Ricardo versus Hélio and Marcela versus Romeo. From the beginning, Victor, using his development, manages to block the action of evil spirits which leaves the fight equal to the advantage of the mutants of good.

Between Ricardo and Helium, despite the latter having power over fire, he cannot have active force against the master of magnetism. The victory of the first occurs quickly. Between Clementine and Victor, the situation is the same: All attacks of the evil mutant are blocked. In an oversight of it, Victor applies a Fatal counterstroke that causes her to fall to Earth. However, Marcela's situation differs because as Romeo has the strength, he can hurt her a little with a blow. She is quickly helped by her boyfriend who gives back on the same coin against Romeo.

The guardians of evil are defeated in this battle. As they are good, the other mutants spare their lives and a few moments later the peasants are freed and put to safety in time.

Effusively, thank you. With the mission accomplished, the soldiers of the good return to Angel's residence. When they get there, they give the good news. They are congratulated and released. Another majority victory against elitist minorities! Keep up, readers.

2.60-PHYSICAL TELEPATHY

Time is advancing fast. Days and weeks pass. It arrives exactly on the day scheduled for the second meeting between healer and Vítor. Early in the morning, the last one, after eating breakfast and arranging the last details, left for Painter's place. That's where your new master's simple shack was.

Along the way, he had the opportunity to revisit those places for the second time since moving to the pompous village of Carabais. It was really something extraordinary that little piece of package. A place very similar to their homeland despite belonging to different regions. He felt, therefore, at home despite not having many close friends, but it was something to be conquered with time.

Regarding the news, you will find two groups of people on the road: hunters and washerwomen. Greet them out of courtesy and both move on. Some venomous animals also seem to require it to deviate a little. Pick up the trail just ahead. At one point in the journey, some forest beings try to get in touch. However, he does not have time to dispense the necessary attention because a mixture of longing, fear, restlessness, and doubt predominate in his being. At the right time, I was hoping to be softened. Probably, after fulfilling a new stage he didn't even know what it would be.

The little dreamer of the backcountry remains delivered into the hands of fate. A while later, it finally approaches the goal. He walks a few more meters and, as he approached the door, he knocks firmly to be attended to. Moments later, he is attended to and kindly the host invites him to enter. Invitation accepted, the two settles in the center of the hut (on stools) standing in front of each other. After a quick exchange of glances, the dialogue finally starts.

"Good morning, Victor. First, I ask you to repeat a short prayer before we begin work. (Healer)

"Yes, of course. I'm all ears. (Victor)

"May good spirits protect us from evil ones. Let nothing and no one get in our way and may we absorb the knowledge poured into this place. (Healer)

"May good spirits protect us from evil ones. Let nothing and no one get in our way and may we absorb the knowledge poured into this place. So be it. (Victor)

"All right. Are you ready for the next step? (Healer)

"I believe so. What's this all about? (Victor)

"It is about developing physical telepathy. (Revealed healer)

"Well, I learned some telepathy from my former master. I can currently have some contacts with spirits. (Victor)

"Can you master the distinction between good and evil spirits? (Healer)

"Not yet. Could you teach me more about this reality? I'm a little confused. (Victor)

"I think it's necessary. Angel is an extraordinary master that must have had his reasons for not entrusting some secrets to you. But let's go in parts.1) Most spirits only approach someone when they are in the same tune, in case of invitation or when the person is weak;2°) Generally, they are spirits that are part of an intermediate plan known as "City of Men". Be prudent not to harm them because they have not yet been judged;3°) Do not be fooled by some who make false predictions and the only goal is to destabilize you. Everything will be clearer to you from now on. (Healer)

"I get it. You can start. (Victor)

The healer rose and led Victor to exactly seven steps ahead. He asked you to sit on the floor. Around it, he lined several statuettes of saints. The dialogue then resumed:

"I'm going to leave you alone. Ask the higher spirits for knowledge through their telepathy. After 30 minutes, meet me at the lake.

That said, the healer walked away leaving the disciple alone. What's next? The still inexperienced disciple would have to fix himself. A little desperate, he began to follow the master's instructions during the suggested time. While as hard as he tried, there was no turning back. Nothing unusual happened despite the special climate caused by the presence of the figurines.

At the end of time, he came out of the hut and walked a little. He met his current master on the shores of the lake. Unlike the first time I had been there, the lake was prepared: covered by an aromatic carpet of flowers. Following the master's instructions, they both knelt. In sequence, the healer prayed a little. At one point, he plunged Victor's head into the waters.

Contact made his mind travel between unknown worlds and past lives in a matter of seconds. Everything went very well until he came across a set of ajar doors that interrupted the visions. Which made him return to reality, and it was necessary to get out of the water. He then returned to the conversation.

"Did everything work out? (Victor)

"Partly yes. However, I noticed that your doors are open. It is necessary to correct this so that you do not suffer anymore. (Explained the healer)

"Can you help me then? (Victor)

"Unfortunately, not in this case. But I know someone who can. Her name is Clotilde Matos, a Carabais prayer. She's very much my friend. Find her as soon as possible. As far as telepathy is, it's settled. (Healer)

"Thank you very much. Can I go? (Victor)

"Yes, you can. We'll meet at the end of next month. Sundays as usual. (Healer)

"That's all right. Closed. (Victor)

"See you later. (Healer)

"See you later. (Victor)

That said, Victor walked away starting the small stretch back satisfied. No doubt, at every step taken, he felt better and more confident to be able to face the power of darkness. For the right and for the right! He stated mentally.

The training was taking effect in all the fields of his life. It was of vital importance in coping with his mission. Since losing his father, he felt more family and social responsibility. With his efforts, he hoped to meet the expectations of those he loved most.

With this goal in mind, complete the journey in a reasonable time. You'd get some rest, pay attention to your wife, and you'd only think about the problems the other day. After all, Sunday is to rest.

A new day came up. Since early days, Vítor and his wife have been taking care of their many things. Among them, household chores, market work and social commitments made throughout the day.

Later, at the end of the work, Vítor remembered the advice of the current master. He then spoke quickly with the woman placing important points about her training. She ended up coming to terms with her. At a later moment, he left searching for this new meeting that promised to be important.

Searching for his goal, asked for information about Clotilde's address to a goal, asked explained how to get there. He appreciates it. The wise man's residence was only two hundred yards from where a right corner was unfolding.

From this moment, with eight minutes of vigorous walking, you arrive in front of the destination. For a moment, it's static. Who would Clotilde be? What powers did you possess? Would it be dangerous to get involved with another mystic? Well, he had no choice but to go ahead and find out what was waiting for him.

Making this decision unconsciously, he moves finally leaning against the door. It beats slightly in it with several blows. Wait a minute. As no one answers, he knocks once again forcefully calling the owner of the house. Immediately, the strategy works because a small woman, a little full and appearing to be old age comes to serve him.

"Young man, what do you want?

"I'm looking for Ms. Clotilde. Is she here? (Victor)

"It's me. Please come in. (Clotilde)

Victor accepts the invitation and follows the hostess. As you enter the house, you notice the great simplicity revealed in every detail on the site. A simplicity extremely similar to that of the healer. One then asks: Did all mystics have that destiny or was it a life choice? Or maybe it was still a punishment imposed by the universe? Think quickly about the case and convince yourself that it was a price to pay for all the wisdom gained.

Inside the house, they walk side by side. After a few steps, they have access to the room and can accommodate themselves to the available stools. Standing face to face his eyes intersect. With his experience and daring, Clotilde begins the dialogue.

"What can I do for you, my son?

"A friend advised me to look for her. I want you to close my spiritual doors because they seem to be open. (Victor)

"All right. This is a serious problem that makes psychics suffer a lot. Do you think I can help you? (Clotilde)

"Yes. How's your treatment? (Victor)

"Through prayer. I pray to cure various evils. However, prayer is only worth it if the person who seeks me has a convinced faith. (Clotilde)

"I get it. After everything I've lived in this life, I believe it's possible. God can use it to helping me. I'm ready, I'm ready! (Victor)

"It's perfect. Just wait a minute, young man. (Clotilde)

She withdrew for a moment heading to the kitchen in short but safe steps. His look conveyed security and professionalism. Upon returning, he brought a little gall between his hands. He got closer and made Victor sit on the floor. Then he untied a tissue attached to his waist and wrapped the visitor's chest.

From this moment on, quietly and discreetly, he began to pronounce incomprehensible words as if they belonged to other languages. Even if he tried, Victor understood nothing. Vaguely, I only heard the following: .... Our............... Sir........... Jesus................. Christ!

Over time, Vítor's mind was relaxing. At one point, he deepened into the depths of his been producing an interesting and impressive reaction. It was as if he was truly knowing himself without masks or obstacles, that is, his weaknesses, doubts, restlessness, fears and hidden mysteries were clearly revealed to him. At this moment of escape, everything led to the belief that what he was looking for was possible: "the encounter between two worlds so disparate".

One more second is set. He enters a kind of trance making his essence go even deeper through the complex intricacies of his personality. Just ahead, he notices a flash that spread light through the opening of doors and windows. Full of curiosity, it advances a little further. When you get very close, something pushes you against opening them closing right away.

It is at this very moment that he awakens beside his benefactor, who opens a wide smile.

"Do you feel better? (Clotilde Question)

Still a little stunned by the experience, Vítor stutters:

"Much better! Did you manage to cure me?

"I did my part. For now, I closed their doors. However, be cautious not to open them again. (Clotilde)

"What do you mean? (Victor)

"Do not invite any spirit to approach, and you will no longer have this problem. (Explained Clotilde)

"I get it. I'm going to try. How much did your work cost? (Victor)

"Well, I don't charge for my gift. But if you want to help me, I'm in need. (Clotilde)

"Take that money. (Victor)

"Thank you, son, God pay you. (Clotilde)

"See you later. (Victor)

"See you later. (Clotilde)

After the farewell, Victor went to the exit. Going over the door, he had access to the street. When he was a good distance away, something made him look back. From the entrance of the house, Clotilde cried out:

"Continue on your path. You will succeed because God blesses good and generous people.

Vítor thanked him with a smile and continued to move on. He exceeded 200 meters and approached his residence. When he got there, he'd rest and enjoy moments with his wife. When they were both tired, they'd sleep.

Another day passed and with each step taken he was more prepared for what fate had in given him. Continue.

262-IMPORTANT DECISION

Every day that happened the relationship between Marcela and Ricardo was consolidated without further mishaps. They were engaged and unlike the couple formed between Vítor and Penelope decided to get to know each other better. They were right. Time helped them put everything in their right place.

Approximately seven months after their colleagues' marriages, in one of their joint leisure activities, the two talked eventually deciding to give a definitive solution to the issue. They scheduled for the next month the wedding in the civil.

Only the communication to the respective relatives was missing. They were waiting for their support in every way.

On the same day, they had a family reunion and had no problems being accepted and understood. From now on, they would begin the preparations for the bash they were going to give to the people closest to them.

2.63-RIDE

The timeline advances and arrives exactly on the day agreed for the meeting of the couple (Vítor and Penelope) with the new friends who were called Adelina Maciel, Celia Alonso and Henrietta Soares.

Like any other day, Vítor and Penelope do their everyday activities during the morning and afternoon. In the evening, they go home for dinner, bathe, wear a beautiful outfit and leave following the guidelines given by them in the quick encounter they had.

In less than ten minutes, they arrive at Adelina's house located on the main street. This was no surprise to anyone because although Carabais was a political-agrarian center it was not as populous as most interior centers of the time.

They then arrive at the door. They hit the same and in a matter of seconds is attended by the hostess. It leads them to the central room where their parents and three other friends were already found, a total of five people.

It's the presentations. Everyone greets each other and the conversation begins in a romantic atmosphere by light of lamps and candles that was the light source of the time.

"You mean you're the famous Victor? (Analice, Adelina's mother)

"Yes, it's me. Thank you for the famous one. I hope to build a new story together with my wife here in this pompous village. (Victor)

"Where are you from? (Itamar, Adelina's father)

"I am from the fishing house while my husband is from the Fundão's place. We met at school, fell in love, got married, got married and thank God we're happy. (Penelope)

"You can see it in your eyes. Congratulations are to be. But tell us, do you like the village? (Asked Adelina)

"In particular, I am having the opportunity to have new experiences, meet interesting people and develop my potential. In short, I'm enjoying it very much. (Revealed Victor)

"I'm enjoying it too, but the obligations of a married woman are not easy to reconcile. (Penelope confessed)

"Welcome to the team. (Kids Analice)

"Women complain, they complain, but we men have to turn in thirty to support the house and endure their bad mood in times of crisis. Isn't that Victor? (Itamar)

"I agree in part. Despite being a beast, my wife is also sweet occasionally. (Praised Victor)

"Thank you, thank you. Does he know you're here? (Penelope)

"More or less. He has confidence in me. (Henrietta)

"Be meticulous not to lose this gift because we all here know how cruel it can be. (Advised Celia Alonso)

"Mine are a little more malleable. (Noted Rosa Garcia, another friend)

"Do you want something to eat or drink? (Offered Analice)

"For me, if you have a juice. (Victor)

"I want water. (Penelope)

"Bring the cake, Mom. (Adeline)

"I love cake! (Celia)

"I just want a small piece because I've had a lot of dinner. (Henrietta)

For a moment, Analice left towards the kitchen. Arriving at the enclosure, he went to prepare the orders. Meanwhile, the others continued to communicate in the room cheerfully. Fifteen minutes later, everything was ready. Then the lady of the house, with a scream, called everyone to attend. Those present went to the scene. Upon arriving, they stood around the table in their chairs starting a great atmosphere of fraternization between them. The snack was then served.

After a brief silence interval, the conversation restarts.

"Henrietta, how are things between your father's command and the mutants of good? (Analice was interested)

"More or less. Between wins and losses. But even though I'm his daughter, I admire the performance of the vigilantes. Henrietta

"I admire it too. (Commented Penelope)

"Does anyone know their secret identity? (Asked Itamar)

"No one. Apart from the speculations, it is known that there are four men and two women. (Celia)

"Well, regardless of who they are, their actions have already shaken the structure of the dominant power. I think it's very healthy. (Adeline)

"I agree. But much still to be achieved. (Complemented Victor)

"How about we form our group? (Suggested Rosa)

"For what purposes? (Penelope was interested)

"For friendship, dignity, and transparency. Apart from the oppressive elite! (Pink)

"I'm in. (Victor)

"Me, too. (Penelope)

"But we have no powers. (Noted Celia)

"You don't have to. A work of raising awareness of those closest to us was enough for our cause. (Pink)

"That's a great idea. You can count on me. What about you, Mom and Dad? (Adeline)

"We don't have the strength or age to do that. Isn't that my old man? (Analice)

"It's true. But you have our full support. (Itamar)

"You have forgotten that I am also an elite. Are you going to fight me? (Grieved Henrietta)

"Don't worry about it. You're the good elite. (Pink)

"Then count on me too. Henrietta

To sign the agreement, the six young men stood up for a moment. They stood in a circle and held hands, they swore they would always be together, be friends, and fight for the cause. In the end, there was a collective embrace with the participation of all.

After the hug, the gifts returned to the table and took care to finish feeding. There were still a few moments of exchanging information. Staying a little later, Vítor and Penelope were trying to say goodbye because they would have hard and exhausting work ahead of them the other day. The other visitors took advantage of the cue and also said goodbye. In a matter of seconds, they left.

Going out together, each sought their fate by promising even separate acting together. Oh, that's good. Now we have more allies against the power of corruption and authoritarianism of that time. Let's move on.

Without further mishaps, the couple Vítor and Penelope came home. They immediately took a night to sleep because they felt exhausted. One more step successfully completed.

2.64-REACTION

As every action has a reaction, the evil mutants after defeat in the last battle tried to find a possible solution to the new imposed situation. To do so, they held numerous meetings together with the chief Lord Soares and Esmeralda, the spiritual leader. They ended up having an idea and organized themselves to put it into practice.

The day chosen fell exactly one day after the tour of the couple Vítor and Penelope. In detail, the following happened: Three mutants were chosen (Henry, Patricia, and Romeo) and were sent to the center of the village to arrest any harmless citizen who got in his way.

That's how it was done. They arrested a boy and a young girl and took them to the dungeon of the farm shouting to the four winds that whoever had the courage to rescue them. With that, this rumor spread fast.

Reaching the ears of the Mutants of good, a reaction was organized. The group consisted of Rafael, Ricardo, and Marcela. All three were invisible and moved without problems until very close to the fortress. When they were detected by their rivals, they had no choice but to face a fight. The hostages were released immediately (They were just bait and had already served their purpose). The pairs of combat formed were: Rafael Versus Henrique; Patricia Versus Marcela; Romeo versus Ricardo.

Between Rafael and Henrique, the dispute proved to be balanced because although the former did not have powers, he had many interesting techniques. Marcela, on the other hand, has a slight advantage over Patricia because with her special ability to read minds, she can predict all the moves of her opponent, facilitating the defense between Romeo and Ricardo, the former has no difficulty in mastering it.

During fifteen minutes of intense battle, the situation does not change. Those disadvantaged end up begging for mercy. The battle, without major losses, is ended with a two-to-one advantage for the mutants of good. It can be said that in a way the attempt had been a failure. Everyone will return to their homes without yet a definition of how this dispute would end.

2.65-HYPNOSIS

Time advances and arrives again on the day marked for the third meeting of mutual spiritual learning between the healer and his disciple, Victor. As always, the latter arrives punctually in the master's hut. When approaching the door, it hits firmly in it three times.

In a few moments it is attended and both enter the hut for another important experience. They move to what the kitchen would be like. In this environment, they sit on the available stools and face each other in front of each other. The master is the first to make conversation.

"How did you get by, Dear Victor?

"Well, what about you?

"In peace. Did you take my advice?

"Yes. You were really right. I'm better now.

"I'm so good. But don't call me Sir. We are friends above all else and dispense with these stupid formalities.

"That's all right. What's today's assignment?

"I'm going to teach you about hypnosis. Are you ready?

"Yes. I am ready for anything and everything.

With the positive response, the healer withdrew from Victor's presence for a moment. Soon after, he returned dressed strictly: white clothes with some tears. Taken a few steps, he came very close to the servant flattening his hands on his forehead. Immediately, he uttered a mysterious prayer for five minutes. After this time, the Healer led him out.

Outside, he began to teach:

See the horizon, Victor? While for us, it is infinite in both directions to God, he is finite. You know, I want to tell you a story known to a few: In ancient times, this region was once an oasis. From here a river flowed into The San Francisco and flowed into the Atlantic. Because of the river, the land was extremely fertile and the population of that time lived quietly abundant. It was a real paradise.

"Right? And why has it turned into this dry region?

"Work of magic. On the coast, there was a master in black magic who, by casting a plague, made the river dry. The only trace of him is the lake. It's exactly in it that you'll learn again. Let's go.

Victor obeyed the master. When he got very close, he was instructed to sit on the banks of it. The healer then explained:

"What I will teach is extremely effective for a person's development. Can I start?

"You can do it.

"Pay close attention to the water in the lake. Describe it.

"It's clear, light-tone and bubbly.

"Look at her and imagine an image that caused her extreme pain or joy. A reminder of your past.

Victor obeyed. After a few moments of concentration, he began to relax. With a little more time fell partly asleep, which gave him the opportunity to start an astral journey. In this kind of relaxing. With some important moments of his life with the company of parents, animals and nature itself. Focusing on each image, gradually was controlling his instincts. This brought as consequences an abundant peace and self-control as well. All his fears and restlessness had lame behind. For a while, he immersed in this direction until he heard a serious and clear voice say: Wake up!

This command was enough to awaken Victor and made him come back to reality. The master then resumed the conversation:

"Tell me your experience.

"I felt a little immersed in myself. Painful memories still cause me enormous pain.

"It was expected. But from now on, you have the tools to move on without trauma just like I did one day.

"What is this technique called again? Hypnosis?

"Yes. But not the common one. A special guy that only I know and should only be used in special cases, understand?

"That's all right. Am I clear? I want to pay attention to my wife.

"It is. You can go now. We meet in a month, at the same time and place. Right?

"Positive.

The two greeted each other and Victor finally left. I'd make my way back. When I got home, I'd take care of his wife like he promised and only think about the other backlogs the other day. Keep up, readers.

The days go by. Every moment the clash between good versus evil, elites versus people, prejudice versus open mind is intensifying. But thank God so far, no tragedy had occurred in the vast region of Pesqueira.

Specifically, relates the main characters, continued preparations for the wedding between Ricardo and Marcela. Esmeralda along with the major planned new actions and Angel continued in the beautiful work ahead of the mutants. He remained calm, though his heart tore from the inside for impossible love. The other mutants continued in the search for development (each defending their position). Regarding the couple formed by Vítor and Penelope, they were living an excellent time both in the personal and professional area.

It was exactly this last item that aroused more and more envy in certain people of the village. This feeling grew so much that one of them began to plan something to hinder the progress of the business commanded by Vítor.

The person I'm talking about was José Pereira. He was a former merchant in the village who owns a bakery, a market, and a bar. For one reason or another, he ended up having to close the business and now lived on small services provided.

Feeling unhappy and disgusted with life, Joseph hired a marginal to do a job. Let's see what happened.

On a normal day of public service, Vítor performed his work in the market when he entered the establishment a slender subject, with few manners and apparently nervous. Next to him, he carried a punch-punch shotgun. Gently, Victor approached.

"What do you want, sir?

"I want a packet of cookies.

"Just a moment. I'll bring it right away.

Victor walked away a little while going to look for the request. Upon finding him, he immediately returned to the initial location. Upon delivering the request, the man pointed the gun in his direction threatening:

"Give me everything you have in the box if you don't want to carry fire.

"That's all right. Just stay calm.

Nervously, Victor headed with the marginal to the cashier. By opening it, he handed over the money available on him. Quickly, the assailant walked away, but always with the gun in his hand. Static, moments later, Victor heard the noise of a horse trot moving away. When he made sure he was safe, he watched outside, but it was too late. It was already out of range.

It had been the worst experience of his life and the scare had been so great that he had not even thought of reacting. But analyzing coldly had been the best choice because despite being a mutant had been taken surprised and any false move his could because for a shot.

With a few minutes, he recovers from the psychological shock. He then closes the doors and heads to the chief's residence. Once there, it reports what happened. In a quick meeting, they decide two things: Report the case at the police station and hire a vigilante.

With the decision made, they will put them into practice. While Angel goes to look for the clerk, Victor goes to the police station.

With a ten-minute walk, Vítor finally arrives at the police station. It is a small building, located at the end of the main street on the right. Quickly, enter the enclosure. He was in the service room where he finds three employees in service: Marcelo Dias (Delegate), Peixoto (registrar) and Tobias Leve (jailer). However, they were in total slouch (Napping) which put everyone from Carabais in Danger. Outraged, Victor gives a shout what is enough to awaken them.

"Who? When? As? (The three babbled)

"I'm sorry if I'm bothering you. It's up to you that I come to report. (Explained Vítor)

"Don't tell me the Cangaceiros attacked him. If that's the case, you've wasted your time because I don't have enough troops to stand up to them. Those bad guys put it on the run to the government. (Marcelo)

"I'm just a clerk. I don't deal with this situation either. (Peixoto)

"Me, too. (Tobias)

"It's not like that at all. I suppose it's simple to solve. (Victor)

"All right? What's this all about? Peixoto, write everything he says. (Wanted to know Marcelo)

"There was a robbery just now in the establishment I work in. A thief took all the recipes for the day. (Victor)

"Could you describe the guys? (Marcelo)

"A tall, thin guy, appearing to be fifty years old, dark eyes and skin. He was carrying a shotgun and a bag. (Victor)

"Have you seen him anywhere else? Did you leave any clues? (Marcelo)

"No, I've never seen him. I was paralyzed with fear and I didn't follow him. (Victor)

"I get it. I'm going to start the investigation, and in case you get anything, I'll let you know. (Marcelo)

"Thank you, thank you. I'll be waiting. See you later. (Victor)

"See you later! (the other three)

Victor has made his way out. Overcoming the obstacle, he assessed the outside. With this, the journey back began. I had done my part, and now I would expect the arrangements made to resolve the matter. When the chief arranged for the vigilante, he would again open the doors of the establishment.

The black day would pass and remain firm in its projects facing everything and everyone.

2.68-WEDDING

Time continues to advance and finally comes the day marked for the marriage relationship between Marcela and Ricardo. From an early age, the bride, and groom prepared in their respective residences. They are only on schedule for civil and religious celebrations.

In an atmosphere of harmony and happiness and with the presence of family, friends and acquaintances, the two-promise eternal unity and love. After the ceremonies, the gifts leave for a reserved club and there begin to celebrate.

For about three hours, between hours, between and drinks everyone has a lot of fun. Until the time comes when, according to tradition, the groom kidnaps the bride and together go on their honeymoon. To be held in the new house, at the fishing house. There begins a new phase in the lives of the two that promised to be quite interesting.

They had followed the example of the couple of friends Victor and Penelope.

2.69-SHOCK

Returning to the dispute between the two groups of mutants, the evil side was not at all satisfied with the outcome of the last battles. To change the current reality, Esmeralda (the leader) promoted several meetings between her commanding. In these hours, it intensified its potential.

When he felt they were ready, he gave each one the pentagon-shaped amulet of darkness. He advised them to wear it in hours of tightening. It was now just necessary to promote a new meeting between the "opposing forces".

The right opportunity arose when the major attempted to occupy land adjacent to his property. Outraged, the owners asked the mutants for help in spreading the word. When they arrived in Angel's ears, he decided to send four of his commanding officers for rescuing the land. The chosen ones were Rafael, Ricardo, Penelope, and Victor.

This team, facing all the adversities of the way, approached the opponents and then the fight was started. It was four against four.

Each caught their opponent getting the distribution in this way: Henry and Penelope; Orlando and Ricardo; Victor and Clementina: Rafael and Patricia. Initially balanced, the dispute was gaining the following contours: Penelope, Ricardo, Vítor and Patricia take advantage over opponents. Consisting of a 3×1 for good. As time passes and the situation does not change, opponents follow the advice and use the magic of the pentagon.

The score turns to 3-1 for evil, except Victor who is immune to magic. Not content with the result, the villain's group continues to massacre the good guys, imposing humiliations. They went so far as to kill the mighty Ricardo Cardoso from a blow to the head.

Disgusted, Victor reacts. With his developed powers he gives back on Orlando, killing him too. That equals the casualties. Soon after, to avoid major disasters, he retires with his colleagues. The battle had been completely lost. The goal had not been achieved. The victory had been the witch's, but at a high cost to both sides. What's next? What would happen?

2.70-NEW MEETING

After the fact, everyone involved engaged in the preparation of the bodies with a view to giving him a decent burial on the same day. Separated, Ricardo and Orlando are buried in the village cemetery with the presence of family, friends, and acquaintances. All tributes are paid to them.

At the end, the remnants of the group of vigilantes commanded by Angel immediately arranged a meeting with the purpose of discussing internal issues of the group. The meeting would be held on the afternoon of the same day.

In the usual place and at the agreed time, all attended and were welcomed by the host who led them to the small room. Each settling in their respective seat.

The first to speak was the master:

"I deeply regret what happened, but we all knew the risks we were taking when we engaged in such a large project. As I do, we keep going. What do you think?

"I am desolate. You know, I lost a wonderful companion while still on my honeymoon. However, I know that his will is that we continue. Let's move on! (Marcela)

"I understand your pain. I've also lost people nearby and admired Ricardo for his power and character. We're together! (Victor)

"I'm here to support whatever it takes. (Penelope)

"It was really traumatic. I've never seen a murder before. But if necessary, I will also donate my life for the cause. For Ricardo! (Raphael)

"Then unanimously it is decided that the fighting continues. Wait just a minute I have a present for each of you. (Angel)

Angel walked away for a moment. He went to his room. About five minutes later, he returned bringing five chains each with a crucifix. He distributed four and got one. Realizing everyone's curious gaze, he explained:

"This symbol will protect us from the attacks. This puts us on equal footing to the advantage depending on our efforts. If we reach the necessary harmony, we can achieve the final triumph.

"Perfect. I admire his story. (Victor)

"I will seek comfort for my pain in your breathing. (revealed Marcela)

"You will find the consolation. I'm sure he'll always support us. (Penelope)

"With our cooperation, it is possible for him to make a difference. (Raphael)

"That's it, guys. We need faith to endure the pain, circumvent obstacles and follow the difficult crossing ahead. I note that you have learned this divinely. To success! (Angel)

Angel's exclamation infects everyone who approached each other resulting in a five-year hug. From contact, a little light is produced represented the strength of friendship.

As they drift away, it dissipates physically, but would always be present in their respective hearts. Vigilantes forever!

Soon after, Angel fires everyone because they had obligations to fulfill. The group's work would only be resumed at the right time. Meanwhile, he'd think about the next steps.

2.71-ABSTRACTION

A few days went by without much news. The day was scheduled for the fourth meeting between the healer and Victor, in the search for the spiritual improvement of both.

As usual, the meeting fell on Sunday. After taking breakfast, Vítor immediately went to his planned destination.

Facing the adversities already known, he fulfilled the total journey in eighteen minutes of vigorous walking. As he got closer to the goal, his heart sped as if he were about to experience unusual and unpredictable experiences. It would probably happen, but it was nothing new because ever since he discovered his gift, young Victor saw his life turn into a Ferris wheel. And what a wheel!

He had already learned about white magic, had entered a group of mutants who had become vigilantes, had lost his father, had been disappointed in love, met Penelope, engaged, married, and was now experiencing knowledge beyond good and evil. He had already convinced himself that anything was possible. For all your loved ones, you'd keep moving forward. At this very moment, you walk a little further. Arriving at the door, he knocks hard then three times. Wait a minute.

The master attends you and initially leads you to the living room. They settle on the available stools and the conversation is finally started.

"How have you been, Victor? Ready for a next challenge?

"Well, thank you. I'm willing to learn more. What's the challenge today?

"I'm going to teach you about abstraction, and I hope you don't get traumatized. Can we get started?

"Yes, of course.

"Follow me then.

Victor obeyed the master following him to the room. The door was locked from the inside in order to avoid unforeseen events. As he felt safe, the healer approached a painting. After a few moments of contemplation, remove him from the wall.

At this time, the student had access to the view of a mirror. Before his expression of doubt, the master clarifies:

"This is my secret mirror. He owns very important properties. Put your right hand on it.

The Servant obeyed once more. To the touch, something fantastic happened: Suddenly, his reflection began to move and come to life. Soon after, he came out of the mirror and stood next to him.

Seeing the disciple's face of astonishment, the healer intervened again.

"Don't be afraid. He's part of you, which means it's you. It's about your yang.

"Yang? What is this?

"Your masculine principle. It also means the light inside. Along with Yin that is the female part complete your being.

"I get it. My old master had told me a little about it. What good is this twin brother to me?

"I'm not a twin. I'm you!

"When you're too busy, you can send it to replace it in simple missions. (Clarified the healer)

"I like that. I'm really busy. (Victor)

"Just don't use me to fool people. (Alerted the lookalike)

"It's true. The substitution has a limit. Anyway, congratulations. You're one of the few mortals who can make yourself ubiquitous. (Healer)

"Thank you, thank you. What's next? How do you reverse the process?

"Tap the mirror again.

Victor again followed the master's instructions. Upon touch, he returned into the mirror. The abstraction was then completed.

"Anything else? (Interested Victor)

"No. You're clear. We'll meet next month, the usual day. (Healer)

"That's all right. See you later. (Victor)

"See you later. (healer)

Victor left the room. He went through the room and overtook the exit. Outside, he took the same old path. Quietly, he would continue his routine activities when he got home.

At the end of the day, he would rest and plan the next steps relating to his personal life. Straight ahead always! In search of fate still uncertain. Would it be all right? Let's keep following the facts.

As Vítor had promised, the delegate Marcelo Dias was committed to the investigation of the theft that occurred in the market. Gradually, he was collecting evidence, making associations and interviewing witnesses. After a careful analysis of everything that had happened, a conclusion was reached about what is most important and responsible for all this: Mister José Pereira.

Certain of his conclusions, Marcelo gathered his commands leaving for the search and seizure of the misapprehension. As everything in Carabais was close, with ten minutes of vigorous walking, the stage coach reaches the goal (residence of José Pereira) and preventively the fence completely.

As commander of the operation, Marcelo is the one who takes the initiative. Approaching the door, he then knocks several times on it firmly. Inside the house, Joseph listens and immediately will answer without even suspecting what awaits him.

The moment you open the door, the deputy announces your arrest. The underlings handcuff him and the individual doesn't even outline a reaction size the state line involving the operation. It is then referred to the police station. Once there, he's interrogated and fined. Even without confessing, you are preemptively arrested for such a number of evidences against you.

The following steps were to send a letter to a judge at the office requesting definitive arrest and communication to the victims of the solution of the problem.

For all his efforts, the deputy was to be congratulated. This time justice had been done. A rarity in an age dominated by authoritarianism, corruption, disputing and social inequalities among others.

As stated earlier, Vítor and Angel were briefed on the results of the investigation. In order to discuss important issues, they scheduled a hastily meeting on the same day.

As agreed, those involved (Vítor and Penelope) attended the head's residence at the scheduled time. After a warm welcome given by the host, they were sent to the room. With the doors of the house properly locked, they began to exchange ideas about the business until then, because of the macabre previous episode.

For three hours, with a vote and time for all, the professional future of those involved was decided to reach a consensus. Some main items were defined: Immediate reopening of the project, beginning of the activities of the hired vigilante (it was called Severino Falcão, local farmer), continued mass dissemination and possible expansion of activities in the future.

After the meeting, they went to take care of their personal affairs and preparations for the reopening that was scheduled to take place the other day. Everything would have to be in the conforms whose main goal was success.

The other day, from an early age, the characters involved take care of all the necessary details that would allow the reopening of the market. In two hours of intense effort, everything is ready.

They make a quick meal. At the end, they propose to start work immediately in a real joint force. The team consisted of four people: Angel, Vítor, Penelope and Severino Falcão.

That's how it's done. The market is reopened and gradually customers and friends are arriving in order to honor this important event. On the other hand, employees strive to provide good service to everyone by offering a wide variety of exposed products.

Throughout the day, the movement continues intense and sales increase by the moment. A short lunch break is given and, on the way, back the work continues. At the end of the day, the office ends with a large positive balance. The reopening had been a resounding success and as planning a portion of the profits would be reinvested in the business itself.

Envy had not brought down these warriors.

2.75-THE ACTION OF THE GROUP OF FRIENDS

The week continued to run normal. Some important facts to highlight: the opposing sides continued in their preparation with a view to new battles; the judge, analyzing the evidence, requested the definitive arrest of José Pereira and had scheduled a trial, Marcela was in the process of recovering from her husband's death; the light market team continued with their intense work; The Torres and Magellan family continued to face adversity with claw at Fundão's Place; And as for the political situation, it remained stagnant. However, the pressures for change increased by the day.

In order to intensify the charges, the friends Celia, Rosa, Adelina met and agreed to start an awareness activity as suggested at the last meeting.

As it was Sunday, they went to the residence of the couple of friends Victor and Penelope in order to invite them to participate as well. The only one who would be left out of this action would be Henrietta who for obvious reasons could not expose herself publicly (After all, she was the Colonel's daughter).

Arriving at the destination, they are well received and go straight to the point. The couple agrees to participate as long as everything is in secrecy. On the opportunity, the latest details are planned and the conditions are accepted.

Soon after, they get out of the house together. As agreed, they will visit the homes of trusted people. In each of them, they give a little lecture. The result of this effort is that they get majority support against the dismembers of the elites in general and would use this trump card at the right time.

At the end of the morning, the work is closed. In order to celebrate, they head to a bar known in the region for their typical dishes. When they arrive at the venue, they settle in chairs around a table right in the center. Evaluate the menu and end up choosing "Couscous with beef jerky". The request is made to the attendant and while they wait, they talk distractedly.

"What did you think of the results? (Adeline)

"It was great. As predicted. I'm glad we decided to put our plans into practice. (Pink)

"You're right and thank you for calling us. You always count on us, don't you, love? (Penelope)

"Yes, of course. We have taken a great step towards real change. (noted Victor)

"Well, I didn't really believe it would work. But I realized that together we're strong. We're to be congratulated. (Celia)

"Now just wait for the right moment for the rebellion to explode. (Adeline)

"When will this be? (Wanted to know Celia)

"Nobody knows. It has to be a very serious fact to generate a general upheave. (Explained Adelina)

"Do you want a more serious fact than the death of two people? I think it lacks courage on our part. (Victor)

"It's not that simple, Victor. The elites still have many allies. (Pink)

"Looking this way, I agree. (Victor)

"Besides, caution doesn't hurt anyone. (Penelope)

"But our day will come. It will have a happy ending if not for everyone, but at least for a good part. (Adeline)

"I'll take it! (Wished Penelope)

The attendant approaches, serves the food and the conversation continues to revolve on several important issues. For three hours, those present have the opportunity to get to know each other better and strengthen ties even closer.

After this time, they say goodbye promising to act again only in serious cases going to end the rest of Sunday in their respective residences. Similar to the group of vigilantes, and inspired by the musketeers, the motto of the group was: One for all and all for one! For the right and fair!

End

CPSIA information can be obtained
at www.ICGtesting.com
Printed in the USA
LVHW051244010421
683211LV00004B/521